The Dancing Doll

T. B. Vera

Published by T. B. Vera, 2018.

This is a work of fiction. Similarities to real people, places, or events are entirely coincidental.

THE DANCING DOLL

First edition. November 28, 2018.

Copyright © 2018 T. B. Vera.

ISBN: 978-1393591634

Written by T. B. Vera.

Table of Contents

Chapter 1..1

Chapter 2..6

Chapter 3..7

Chapter 4..9

Chapter 5...13

Chapter 6...15

Chapter 7...19

Chapter 8...24

Chapter 9...27

Chapter 10..31

Chapter 11..33

Chapter 12..36

Chapter 13..40

Chapter 14..42

Chapter 15..44

Chapter 16..46

Chapter 17..48

Chapter 18..50

Chapter 19..53

Chapter 20..56

To Ms. Horgan my AP English teacher, who first influenced my wanting to become a better writer; and Professor Henry, Professor Barkin, and Professor Oppenheimer, who cleared the fog and helped me to start thinking and learning outside the system.

Chapter 1

1845

The Bromwells were one of the wealthiest families in West London. They lived in an old gothic-revival style mansion; an ancestral home which emitted its own quality of shadowy grace, like the terrifying beauty of an irate ocean wave. It was a place which housed many rooms, and even more secrets.

The Bromwells' fortunate lifestyle was the result of a clothing company by the name of Bromwell's Best. It had been passed along to each rising generation, and was now in the hands of Bane Bromwell. Compared to his predecessors, Bane Bromwell did not follow the rules, he made them.

He based his clothing designs on images that he dreamt up, resulting in a fantastically original style. He prided himself on using materials that were functional as well as fashionable. And he sold his products at mind-bogglingly competitive prices.

Bane Bromwell thrived, not only in his business but in life, because he carefully kept his most important affairs private and within his family.

His wife was Devona Bromwell. She had shocking eyes, like suffocating, frigid depths; and with her tame touch her abundance of golden waves was always perfectly placed. Unlike many women, she was not squeamish when presented with a grisly ordeal. When she was a child, she entertained herself by cutting off the heads of small animals and sewing them back on to mismatched bodies, keeping her favorite experiments as monstrous trophies.

Devona made sure that the house was kept in order. It was her duty to discipline the servants should they fail, something she enjoyed with a sickening satisfaction.

The Bromwell boys were Avery, Delmar, and Zackarias.

Avery was grown, and worked for his father as the head of his security team. His muscles were thick like interwoven vines, and he seemed to revel in the destruction of the human body. He had proven himself hazardous more than once, but it was not his strength that was feared so much as the power behind it; power which only those who were unlucky enough found themselves facing.

Delmar was eighteen and a Master of Music, especially with his violin. When he played, one could not help but listen. His fluid fingers caressed the strings in a motion that was itself a work of art. Delmar at times used his musical prowess to inflict pain on people, forcing them to commit bizarre and repulsive acts.

Zackarias was the youngest Bromwell boy, and, like his father, was used to getting his way. He loved to read, especially books about viruses, poisons, and chemical reactions. He mixed his own brand of concoctions as leverage to bend people to his will.

And of course, the youngest child and only girl: Celise Bromwell.

Unlike most children, Celise did not spend her time casually demanding attention. She preferred to operate independently and in the shadows.

· · · ·

MR. BROMWELL'S OFFICE was in the back parlor of the mansion. It was two-and-a-half stories tall. The rooftop was a great sealed spiderweb of spikes to discourage birds and small animals from perching. Hanging from the ceiling was a rock crystal chandelier, over six feet in diameter at its widest point, and five feet tall.

"Please, Mr. Bromwell, will you just think about it?" Victor Nusánce, Mr. Bromwell's business manager was saying.

"Imagine how much more you could accomplish by taking a deal like this. There will be no limit to the diversity and distribution of your products and services. With their added resources, you would be prepared in just a few years to introduce your line overseas. Think about the connections you could gain. And the more people you know, the more people will know about *you*," Mr. Nusánce said in a sly, unpleasant tone.

Mr. Bromwell put his head in his hands and released an irritated sigh.

Ivan Bilson and Park Tanner of Bilson and Tanner's Clothing House were Mr. Bromwell's top competitors, but in the last year they had been having a poor time keeping up with sales. As delivered by Mr. Nusánce for days non-stop, they had devised a partnership deal to keep their business alive, and perhaps gain insight from such a discerning businessman like Mr. Bromwell.

He clasped his hands and looked at the hated document that had been placed on his desk. Bromwell's was a family operation, and this was not about to change.

Besides, Victor Nusánce was greedy and impatient, always looking to forward his own agendas. Truthfully, Mr. Bromwell disliked him immensely, but the expertise which he usually demonstrated convinced Mr. Bromwell to hold onto him – at least until he could find a replacement.

"Mr. Nusánce, I have told you - I don't know how many times - how I feel about this offer-"

"I understand, sir, but-"

"And since you are not only wasting my time, but giving me a headache, I see no point in continuing this nonsense. Now, if you value your position, I command you to forget about this joke of a proposal and focus on important business matters: *Mine.*"

Mr. Nusánce scrunched up his face, looking angry and disgusted. Throughout his life he had been a servant to others, always having to answer to someone else's call, but he intended to end the cycle here. This deal would be the start of his reign, and once it was complete he would arrange an accident for Mr. Bromwell; then seizing control from Bilson and Tanner would be an elementary game.

"Mr. Bromwell . . . I am *begging* you," -the word oozed from his throat like a thick sludge- "take the deal. It is the most profitable investment you are ever likely to be presented with. And though it is based on a partnership, we both know who would truly be in command." Mr. Nusánce spoke those last words like he knew a delicious secret. "Mr. Bromwell, I-"

"Daddy?"

Mr. Bromwell looked past Mr. Nusánce to see his daughter standing in the doorway. He had forgotten to shut the door.

"Hello, Celise. What is it?"

Celise stepped into the room and asked, "Daddy, may we talk?" Mr. Bromwell looked confused. "Delmar and Zackarias are busy and told me no. And I'm bored, and right now I don't want to be by myself."

Celise was seven years old. She wore a dark blue dress with a short cascade of ruffles, and gray stockings that matched her little black boots. Her black, wavy hair was pinned back on the right; and her eyes glinted like sapphires. Her favorite plain gray satchel was slung over her left shoulder.

Mr. Nusánce was repulsed. He despised children; and Mr. Bromwell's daughter, with her serious, piercing stare made him uncomfortable.

"Celise, why don't you go find your mother," Mr. Bromwell said. As much as he couldn't stand having to deal with Mr. Nusánce, he certainly had no spare time to spend in casual conversation with his daughter.

Celise sighed like she had been expecting this. "Mother suggested the same thing about you. But one of the maids broke a vase in the dining room and she had to punish her, and you know how that is." Mr. Bromwell did indeed. With the successes of his business came spies and thieves trying to copy and sell his work; naturally, they had to be dealt with.

Damn you, Devona, he thought. Like she wasn't aware of how much he already had to manage. His thoughts were interrupted by a pulling sensation. Celise was climbing onto his lap.

She stared at Mr. Nusánce and though her lips never moved, her eyes were scathingly critical.

Mr. Nusánce stared back, not bothering to hide his loathing. He turned his attention back to Mr. Bromwell and said, "Mr. Bromwell, may we continue our meeting?"

Mr. Bromwell sighed again, this time as if to say: *Are you stupid?*

"There is *no* meeting, Mr. Nusánce. And since you have nothing relevant to say-"

"Oh no, Mr. Bromwell," Mr. Nusánce said. His voice had adopted a sinister edge. "We are *not* finished here."

Mr. Bromwell's voice turned lethal as he said, "Leave now, Nusánce, while you still have your job *and* your life."

Mr. Nusánce stayed where he was. He reached into his coat and pulled a pistol from a concealed pocket, then pointed it at Mr. Bromwell. There was a *click*, followed by a musical crash.

Mr. Bromwell was still for a few moments. He carried Celise as he stood and leaned over his desk to observe the mess of flesh, bone, and chandelier on his otherwise perfect floor. Mr. Nusánce's hand, still holding the gun, was no longer attached to his arm.

"Well . . . At least that shut him up." Mr. Bromwell looked at the new hole in the ceiling. "Hmm, decrepit framework, I suppose."

Celise's eyebrows met in confusion.

"Daddy, it wasn't the framework. It was me."

Chapter 2

MR. BROMWELL SPLUTTERED. "Celise, don't be stupid. How could you-" he stopped, recalling as if from a distant dream words that his wife had confided in him, something about a special bloodline. He looked intently into his daughter's eyes, like he was trying to find answers to questions he didn't even know he had.

"My darling girl," he finally said, "it was you, wasn't it? Well, you have done me a great service, more than you know. I was planning to replace him but . . ." Mr. Bromwell shrugged, like it made no difference.

"Now, what would you like as a reward? Name anything at all in this entire world that you desire and you will have it."

Celise's eyes grew slightly bigger. She reached into her satchel and pulled out her only cherished treasure: A little black music box decorated with carved images of snakes. When she opened it, a tiny dancer in a shimmering white Romantic Tutu rose and made several revolutions to a melody like falling snow.

Celise looked at her father and said, "This. I want *this*. I want to be a dancer."

Mr. Bromwell scoffed as he said, "Is that all? Then I shall enroll you into the finest dance academy in West London." Seconds later, Mrs. Bromwell burst into the room.

"What happened?! I heard-" She took in the scene.

"It seems, Devona, that Victor has had a, umm, accident."

Mrs. Bromwell stepped closer and examined the carnage. "But . . ." She looked up, her gaze drawn to her daughter's face, and whispered, "I knew it."

2017

Edit Samuel was not ordinary. Not ordinary because he never liked to settle for the framework of his daily routine. He woke up and prepared for his day like many, but sometimes he would literally roll himself out of bed, or rearrange things in the kitchen while making breakfast, just so something was different.

To many, Edit's actions would seem insignificant and a little ridiculous - after all, his day would go on, same as always, and he'd have to wake up and do it all over again - but for Edit, these minute tasks offered some comfort against the unbearable monotony that had settled on his budding life.

· · · ·

TODAY WAS WEDNESDAY, June 21st. Today was Edit's day off, and his birthday.

He was now twenty-four but already felt like 200. He could never find it in himself to be enthusiastic about birthdays anymore, especially his. Since the year he had turned fifteen, they had become less fun, less manageable, more of a hassle than a celebration; and he was just too tired to surround himself with people he had rarely seen or spoken to since middle school.

What to do then? Watching T.V. wasn't really an option, and the concept seemed almost as old and overdone as he felt. Besides, the stuff on T.V. these days was so over-the-top ridiculous – an insult to the shows of his cherished childhood.

There was that charcoal piece he was working on, a landscape style piece of his workplace; although he really didn't feel like sitting still for hours at a time.

Edit turned his attention to his coffee table, one of many gifts from his parents when he was just starting out on his own, and his eyes caught the corner of a beautiful colored pencil piece he had placed in a folder. He smiled when he saw it.

He reached for the folder and opened it, uncovering a child's drawing. It was a gift from Mira, a reminder of their epic snowball fight from last winter. Most of the kids had been sick that day, so there hadn't been much for the caregivers to do but watch them sleep. Mira had been feeling cranky and bored, so she and Edit had gone out for some air. They trekked through the soft crystal-like powder to the park, where they had chucked each other with snowballs all afternoon.

Edit meant to frame the drawing, but he still hadn't found the right frame. He wanted it to be something that he and Mira would both appreciate.

Anyway, he knew now what he wanted to do. He would drop by for a visit at Harlow's; Mira's drawing had reminded him of some business there.

Chapter 4

EDIT WORKED AT A HOME at Harlow's, an adoption agency created by Athena, Artemis, and Aphrodite Harlow. The Harlow sisters had been adopted by Edit's grandmother after their own parents had been trampled by a disconsolate elephant on a zoo trip. They had given Edit his first employment opportunity the year he turned old enough to start working, and were more like his aunts than his bosses.

When Edit knocked on the door, his friend and co-worker Lucy answered.

"Hi, Edit. What are you doing here?" she asked, surprised but happy to see him. Edit stepped inside and the two walked down the hallway into the living room.

"Oh, you know, just thought I'd come by and see my favorite people, seeing as I'm not busy today."

"Uh, yeah you're not busy. It's your day off. And your birthday." Edit groaned. "Anyway, have a seat," Lucy said. "I'll let Athena know you're here. Even though, you know, you shouldn't be."

Edit chuckled and went to greet the kids.

• • • •

"HEY, GUYS," HE SAID, unable to stop the tender smile that illuminated his face. He got down on one knee to pass out hugs and high-fives, and he didn't leave anyone out. Many of the children at Harlow's needed some level of special care, usually a result of their debilitating past experiences.

Eden had severe digestive troubles. Before he had been brought to Harlow's, he had been living in an abandoned construction site. Anything that his grubby little hands could snatch up became food; strips of wood, grime from old equipment, even the dirt from the hard-packed, dusty ground he slept on. Eden had to eat a specific diet to keep his digestive system stable, but sometimes he would relapse and become sick, throwing up for hours.

Reyna had been born with schizophrenia, which caused her to believe she was an animal. She felt inclined to make animal sounds, walk on all fours, leave excrement in inappropriate places, and lash out if she felt threatened.

Carter had been living in an alley for nearly two years. On the night he was found, someone had beaten him up and slashed his face. The physical scars had healed, but their absence only made way for the emotional scars. Carter rarely let people touch him, and he hardly ever spoke. He had been diagnosed with PTSD and was prone to panic attacks.

Then there was Mira. It wasn't fair to the other kids for Edit to choose favorites, but Mira was his; it was he who had found her when he was seventeen years old.

. . . .

IT WAS A QUIET AFTERNOON. Edit decided to take out the trash before reading to the kids. When he stepped into the alley, his ears perked up to the feeble sound of a baby's pained cries. He ran to find the source.

He was heartbroken by what he saw: Someone had dumped the baby on a heap of garbage bags at the end of the alley. She looked thin, and her golden-caramel skin seemed dull, but she was clean and unmarked; no claw or bite marks from rats or anything. Edit picked her up and she began to struggle in his arms, like she was unhappy at being touched.

"Shh," Edit said. "You're okay now. It's okay, little baby. You're . . . You're mine now. You're safe." And the baby, at the sound of the kind, soothing voice stopped crying.

Since that day, Edit had always thought of Mira as his daughter; and Mira had grown to love him as her favorite caregiver. He was the closest thing she had to a parent.

• • • •

MIRA WAS NEVER AS TALKATIVE as the other kids, but she always talked to Edit; sharing secrets, dreams, and most curiously of all, warnings of danger.

"Hey, little sunflower," Edit said, lifting her into a hug.

Her curly, blonde-brown hair brushed his face. She giggled and said, "I thought you weren't coming in today. Artemis told me so."

"Well, I can leave if you want," Edit said, turning in the direction of the door.

"No, no," Mira said, giggling again.

Edit chuckled and sat down in one of the armchairs. He looked up as he noticed Lucy returning with her news.

"Athena says you can stay if you want, but she doesn't want you working. This *is* supposed to be your day off."

A jumbled sound of crashing metal boomed out of the kitchen. Lucy sighed and hurried off to see who had done what.

"Yeah, good luck with that," Edit called after her. "So where is Athena?" he said to Mira. "Actually, where's anyone?"

"Well, Athena is helping Reyna to use the toilet. Aphrodite and Artemis are shopping for groceries. Ellis is getting us some new clothes and books. Ambrose is getting Julian a new mattress, because spiders laid eggs in his. . . ." Mira said with a creased brow. "So that just leaves Lucy and Barry."

"Oh. . . ." Edit said, trying to figure out the spider comment. "Okay, cool."

He shifted in his seat and realized that he was still wearing his backpack. "Wait a minute," he said, "almost forgot what I came here for." He opened his backpack and pulled out a folder like the one on his coffee table. Inside was a portrait of Mira that he had done with watercolors. He had replicated her goofy smile and wild hair beautifully, and her brown, kaleidoscopic eyes were complimented by a border of rainbow-colored flowers.

Mira gasped like her breath had been stolen by an angel. "This is so *awesome*," she said. She held the portrait in one arm and hugged Edit with the other.

He hugged her back and said softly, "You're welcome."

There was a knock on the door, heavy and slow, which sounded out of place in the playful atmosphere.

Barry hurried out from the kitchen, where he and some of the kids had been trying to make chocolate smore cookies. "Hey, dude," he said when he saw Edit. "Wait, you're not supposed to be here."

"That's what people keep telling me."

Barry shook his head and hurried on to the door. Mira gasped as if a corroded metal rod had pierced her lungs.

"Mira?" Edit shook her gently. Her eyes were wide with fear, and except for her trembling lips she was completely still.

"Mira? Mira!"

The other kids in the room noticed the change, and were peeling away from their activities to stare at Mira. At the same time Barry opened the door, then everyone heard him gasp.

"Holy freaking . . . *Athena!*" he yelled at a level he could not control. "Get in here, quick!"

Chapter 5

THE URGENCY IN BARRY'S voice made Edit stand up cautiously. Lucy, the remaining kids, and Athena ran into the living room.

"You'll be okay now," they heard Barry saying. "Everything will be okay." When Barry stepped out from the hallway he had one arm placed gingerly around the shoulders of a little girl, and was gently walking her into the room.

Her long dark hair was matted and bloody, and blank sections of her scalp were replaced by large cuts. Her midriff and arms were exposed by an ensemble of tattered fabric. Her pale skin was blacked out by the layers of dirt that coated her. What did stand out were the lacerations and bruises tattooing her body, colored in volcanic reds and sickly purples. Her skeleton was prominently outlined by her emaciated flesh; and with such a frail frame it was truly a wonder that she could stand at all. On the right side of her mouth, halfway to her ear, was a gash so horrific it exposed some of her teeth. Her lips were swollen and bleeding, and her nose was just a lump on her face.

"Barry, call the hospital! Lucy, keep the kids in their rooms! You and E. will stay and look after them while we . . ." but Edit barely heard Athena. He felt like he might collapse, or vomit, or both. The only thing keeping him steady, as steady as he could be in that moment, was the weight of Mira in his arms. There were bright, plump tears tracing paths down her face.

Edit knew that he needed to be strong, for Mira and the other kids, but in the next few seconds his focus was shifted.

It was as if a malignant force had slithered into the room and taken possession of the girl. She turned her head and stared deliberately at Edit. Her eyes were enticingly deadly; they blazed like a neon blue flame and filled Edit with unpleasant sensations. He wanted to fight and flee, cower and kill, all at once. And just when he thought he would literally die from the fire those eyes possessed, the girl passed out.

Barry caught her in an awkward hot-potato motion, afraid to aggravate her vulnerable condition.

· · · ·

THE PARAMEDICS ARRIVED quickly, and in a few moments the girl was strapped to a gurney and on her way to the emergency room, Athena and Barry close behind her.

The silence after their departure was a heavy one; a thick, black layer which consumed everything in its grip. Several of the kids were crying; so was Lucy. Edit walked over to her and hugged her with his free arm. Mira had stopped crying but was now looking sick and ghostly.

As for Edit, all he could think about was that glare. He would never forget the way it paralyzed his soul and froze the blood in his veins.

Chapter 6

CELISE WAS ELEVEN YEARS old when she began getting into trouble.

True to his word, on the very day of Mr. Nusánce's death, Bane Bromwell enrolled his daughter into the finest dance academy in West London: The Sícone Dual-Spirit Dance Academy. She progressed quickly in her training, earning a spot in the Young Advanced class in under a year, and attracting the attention of Rupert Sícone himself.

Rupert Sícone was a manager for the promotion of the Performing Arts. He worked diligently to form new talents, helping people to not only find their places in the entertainment world, but in life. The only thing he expected in return was his clients' best representations of themselves, and it seemed to him that Celise had been blessed by Terpsichore herself.

Her body seemed naturally adapted for the demonstration of proper technique. Her lines were complete and fluid, highlighting her entire form; and her extensions well-positioned and sustainable. She had a turn value that was athletic, precise, and constant, and acquired such height in her leaps that she appeared to glide through the air. Her flexibility was as natural as that of a contortionist. But what would really serve her well was the fullness in heart which she displayed for her craft.

Celise was a vision, this could not be denied, but at a place like Sícone's she was not the only one.

Sobrina May had been training at Sícone's since the age of two. The drive she had developed for her art helped her to advance almost effortlessly in everything that she did. She was simultaneously awed and envied by many of the dancers, so when Celise was introduced so rapidly into the Young Advanced class, Sobrina disliked her immediately.

• • • •

TODAY'S END-OF-CLASS practice combination was a four-corner à la seconde, followed by a triple front attitude, into four coupé jetés, ending in a ninety-degree first arabesque.

Unfortunately for Sobrina, she was so concerned with out-performing Celise that her attitudes were wobbly, she missed a coupé jeté, and stepped so roughly on her arabesque that she nearly fell over. Whispers and titters rippled through the class, but Madame Delancy was not amused.

"Miss May," she began in a controlled tone, "that was atrocious, especially given your level of training. I don't think you could have disgraced yourself more if you had been a blind hippo." A few more titters.

"You always make such a point to demonstrate your superiority, so I would think you may want to conduct yourself as a *dancer.*" Sobrina kept silent, her eyes shamefully intrigued by the floor.

"Go! And tomorrow I expect you to come prepared!"

"Yes, Madame Delancy. . . ."

Sobrina stepped aside to allow the next girl her turn, and that's when Madame Delancy said loudly, "Miss Bromwell, step forward and demonstrate to Miss May the *proper* exercise."

Celise as per usual was perfection, even earning a compliment from Madame Delancy, a rare occurrence. Sobrina watched, grumbling things under her breath.

Before Celise had shown up it had been she who was asked to demonstrate, she who earned rare compliments; now, Sobrina more often found herself dancing in Celise's background – a backup, an understudy.

Dance was the one thing in Sobrina's life that made her feel truly extraordinary and content, and she refused to give it up – for anything, for anyone.

It was time to end this.

· · · ·

THE YOUNG ADVANCED class was held on the third floor, and Celise was beginning her descent when someone grabbed her shoulder and she was violently spun around.

"You know what, Celise? I've dealt with plenty of girls like you, and you don't intimidate me one bit. Everyone may think that you're a great dancer – amazing – *perfect!* – but I know exactly what you are. And I've been dancing long enough to know that you don't belong here. When you really need to impress, when it really matters the most, you won't be able to handle yourself. *You! Will! Fail!* Better for you to leave now and save yourself the embarrassment."

Speaking of embarrassment, Celise thought. "Sobrina, while unfortunate for you that you messed up your combination, I thought you were at least smart enough to know that it wasn't my fault. I think you should take it as a lesson to concentrate on your dancing, then you won't have to worry so much about trying to beat me."

Celise leaned her face in so that it was just an inch away from Sobrina's. "And you don't intimidate me either."

The rest of the girls had started to gather on the staircase, having heard Sobrina's initial outburst. They stood whispering and giggling, mainly about how red and puffed her face looked.

When Celise tried to walk away, Sobrina stepped down so that she blocked her path.

"Ha! Like I need to try to beat you. The moment I stepped into this building I have been the best dancer in the Young Advanced class. I worked for my spot, but you're allowed in because your daddy donated clothes to the academy."

Celise blinked in surprise and clenched her jaw, and Sobrina looked triumphant at having finally made a scratch in the armor of the perfect little pretender.

It was true that Celise's father had developed a dancewear line exclusively for Sícone students, but Sobrina's statement was just that, based only on her envy.

When Celise spoke, there was the trace of a threat in her tone. "I'm here because I worked hard to be here, the same as you – the same as everyone else. It's not my fault that you're so fixated on beating me that you make an ass of yourself, become an embarrassment to the rest of us, and an insult to Dance. I'm not here so that you can have an excuse for your failures. I'm here to dance!"

Sobrina stood there, mouth agape, looking very much like Celise's perception of her. Celise stepped around her and walked away.

Sobrina was so still that she could have been mistaken for an inanimate object. None of the girls had ever spoken to her like that. She recovered slowly from her shock, like she was processing a realization, then jumped straight into rage.

Screeching like a banshee she tore after Celise, aiming to grab her hair. Celise stepped aside and pointed her left foot toward the banister; Sobrina tripped – hard – and crashed into it. She grabbed it to steady herself, but it jolted violently and began a series of rapid crackling sounds. The banister made some heavier jiggling movements, then it gave way, dropping Sobrina three stories below into empty air.

The stairway was a contorted chorus of terrified screams. People dotted on the different levels glimpsed Sobrina coming down, like she was being pushed by an invisible hand. It happened so swiftly, but it felt like a lifetime.

Celise leaned forward and looked into the hollow surrounded by the lengthy stairway. She saw a jerking heap, each minute the center of a frantic, growing crowd.

She stepped away and walked undisturbedly down the stairs to the carriage waiting for her outside.

Chapter 7

AFTER THE CHANDELIER crash Mrs. Bromwell led her daughter upstairs to her own private room on the top floor.

It was old, small, and almost bare. A row of three tiny windows lined the top-left wall, and a simple two-person sofa sat beneath them. Across from this was a bookcase that spanned two-thirds of the wall, yet there was just one book on the middle shelf. Mrs. Bromwell retrieved it and took a seat; Celise did the same.

"Celise, over three centuries ago, our family – that is, the Adair bloodline, became blessed with a remarkable gift, the same gift which helped you to drop the chandelier. And we owe everything that we are to your eleven-times great-grandmother." Mrs. Bromwell handed the book to Celise. Written inside the front cover were the words: *This book contains the life and tales of Scarlett Daphne Clemens Beaumont Adair.*

Mrs. Bromwell directed Celise to a specific entry, and she began to read.

. . . .

1539,

There was a cold softness at my back. I felt like I was floating. I could tell through my closed eyelids that it was nighttime. I opened my eyes slowly and felt them sting with pain. Every part of me throbbed with the feeling, as if spiders were burrowing into my skin.

Suddenly I remembered everything, and the memories came swarming at me, bombarding my vision. I sat up slowly, the throbbing beginning to subside, and looked around me. I was still in the valley, but I was alone.

Nneka and her mother were gone.

I met them seven days ago.

Mother and I were heading to the market, when I overheard our neighbors talking about two odd strangers who had shown up in the old, forgotten valley.

I couldn't believe it. People rarely came by our village, and when they did they were always so banal. When I asked Mother about the strangers she became angry and told me to keep away, but her warning only made me more curious.

I faked a sickness and told her that I needed to go home. When I got there, I made my way around the back and began the trek up the hill. When I reached the top, I got down on my stomach and looked over the peak. And there they were! Two strangers: a woman and a little girl. They had set up a tent which looked like it could fit about ten people, and were busy setting up their belongings.

While I was watching them, I must have bumped a pebble or done something else to make myself known, because in a moment they both turned to look at me. The woman had a wild, accusing look, but the small girl looked fearful.

I became frozen, as if my body had merged into the hillside. I cursed myself for not having been prepared for an encounter. The woman was the first to speak, and her commanding voice rooted me even more to my spot.

'Who are you? What do you want? How dare you intrude upon the lodgings of a Priestess!'

I couldn't speak.

'Answer me!' She picked up a long, pointed weapon. That did it.

'I . . . I'm Scarlett. I live just down the hill. I-I heard there were newcomers. I wanted to see if this was true. . . .' I knew I must have sounded pathetic in the presence of those fierce-looking warriors, and I was sure the woman would have killed me right then.

Instead, she scrunched up her face, like she was thinking carefully about something. She lowered her weapon and called me closer. I scrambled down into the valley, terrified but excited, and stood right in front of her. She was taller than I had realized, and much more imposing up close. She had broad, graceful shoulders, and a face that looked like it had been sculpted by the most skilled artist. I remember how muddled my thoughts became whenever I stared into her mesmerizing brown eyes. Her arms were decorated with bracelets, and her beautiful dark skin painted with colorful markings.

She held my face, which was unexpected but I let her. She looked into my eyes and I felt my soul ripple with the intensity.

'All right, then,' she said, more to herself I think. 'You may stay if you like.' Then she walked away and continued to arrange her things. I was left with the little girl. We smiled awkwardly for a time, but she no longer seemed afraid.

She told me that her name was Nneka, *which means:* My mother is supreme. *She pronounced it like nay-kuh. Her mother's name was* Yejide, *which means:* Image of the mother, *and was pronounced yeh-jee-deh.*

Nneka told me that they were originally from Yoruba; but their land had been invaded, their people enslaved and taken to a place called Saint-Domingue.

'How did you get here?' I asked her.

'We were guided here by the Lwa *– Spirits. We worship the* Petwo.*'*

She told me that these were aggressive spirits who lived in an invisible world called Ginen. *She told me that people are also spirits, but we live in the visible world. Her words sent thrills throughout my body, as if I had woken up to find myself falling from a great height - but was happy.*

I asked her about the drum she carried. She explained that she was a ritual drummer for her mother, who had been a priestess in their village until-

'Until what?' I asked her.

'Never mind. . . .'

I stayed with them for those seven days. Nneka taught me about the different spirit worlds, and about the spirits of deceased ancestors. She told me that she and Yejide served these spirits in exchange for protection.

On my last day with them, Yejide pulled me aside and spoke very seriously. It was the second time that I had ever felt truly afraid of her; still, I wanted to hear what she had to say.

'Scarlett, I must ask something great of you. Nneka told you that we worship spirits to gain their help and protection, but I knew that there were forces who could provide much more than this. I called on the Petwo. I let them inhabit my body so that we could communicate. They blessed me with extraordinary power, but . . . I am cursed as well.

'I had to sacrifice my husband, and my first two children to accept their gift. I have done wonderful things, but my body has become weak, and with each communication I come closer to joining them. I have lost the strength to wield this gift on my own, and I need someone to carry it on for me. Do you understand what I am asking you, Scarlett?'

'Yes! I'll do it!'

• • • •

IN THEIR TENT, YEJIDE and I sat facing each other, while Nneka sat off to her mother's right, her drum in place. In the middle of the tent, Yejide had placed a wooden pole decorated with images of writhing snakes. It connected the top of the shelter to the grassy landscape.

'Scarlett, any great deed requires a great sacrifice. Once you accept, you can never go back.'

'I accept.' I was aware that I would face unpleasant consequences, although I wasn't sure how I knew; what I did know is that I didn't belong in my old life, and I was ready to begin a new one.

Yejide started to pray, calling on the Petwo, asking them if they would take me into their care, while Nneka struck her drum, releasing a pattern of ancient sounds.

Except for the rhythmic beats, all was quiet for a long time. After Yejide finished her prayers she remained unmoving, and I began to wonder if she was still there. I was becoming worried that the Petwo would not accept me, when the quiet became silence; this time as the result of Nneka's ceased drumming.

I looked at her and saw that she had become as stationary as her mother. Her eyes were wide with surprise, then they rolled back into her head and she collapsed. I turned back to Yejide, shaken, but she seemed unaffected.

I felt something starting to take hold of me, as if a savage wind was pushing me from all sides; wrapping around my skin, burrowing into my heart. It was suffocating me.

Yejide sat like a rock for another minute, then her body heaved upward as if something had been ripped from her chest; it knocked me down, and when I woke up I was alone in the valley.

I decided that the only thing left to do was to go back home to Mother. I stood up and looked around the valley one last time, then turned away and walked despondently back to the village.

• • • •

I WENT UPSTAIRS TO Mother's room and knocked on her door. When she did not answer, I quietly let myself in. She was in her bed, sleeping of course, but there was something else. Even from far away I could see how ghostly pale her skin was.

I ran to her side and shook her. She did not wake. I called her repeatedly, but she ignored me. I felt her face, her skin was stiff and cold. I was struck by such a feeling of horror that it chilled my bones. Then I remembered Yejide's words.

I was sorry for Mother, but the remorse and fear were subsiding. I started to feel excited. I was noticing that I did feel stronger, more awake, like I had been reborn with a wealth of insight. I packed up my meager belongings and left that place forever, and am now on a path to discover my newly awakened self.

Chapter 8

HARLEY BRYSEN WALKED out of the Cornerstone pharmacy with a new box of her favorite ibuprofen brand. She walked to her car in the large parking lot; it was getting dark, and she almost didn't see it tucked away in its corner spot. She dug into her pocket for her keys, but lost her grip and they tumbled onto the pavement. "Ughh," she groaned.

She crouched and got her keys, then paused, waiting for the pain in her back to ease. As she stood, she noticed a flutter of movement some feet away. She positioned her keys between her fingers for a makeshift set of brass knuckles. She was tired and in pain, and wasn't in the mood for anyone's games, but when she looked up she saw a kid. A little girl.

Harley relaxed, but only for a second. *What's she doing in a parking lot by herself?* she wondered. She eyeballed her.

The girl was small, probably eleven or twelve. She wore a black, long-sleeved skirted leotard, black tights, and black ballet shoes. She wasn't doing much, just staring at the ground and walking in small circles. Had she gotten separated from her parents? There were no other people around, and no one in the pharmacy had seemed worried about a lost child.

Whether it was for herself or for the little girl, Harley began to feel nervous. She was about to walk back to the pharmacy and ask for help, but something stopped her. Her legs felt like jelly, her feet glued to the pavement. She leaned against her car to steady herself, and when she looked up again the girl had started dancing.

She took a step forward on the toe of her left foot, then started off with a short set of turns. She switched and balanced in a pose on the toe of her right foot, then followed up with a leap as high as the roof of Harley's car.

"Wow," Harley whispered. It was so unexpected that she just stood and watched; but she would have to get going soon, her back was starting to fall into its discomfort stage. At the same time her bones began to ache, as if they could no longer support her body; and she felt like her organs were being squeezed. She became so weak that she fell to the ground as she tried to rest on one knee. All the while, the girl continued to dance, traveling lightly on her feet and moving her body fluently.

Harley's heart seemed to beat a path out of her chest. "What is this-" she began, but stopped when her heart exploded. Her head lolled to the ground as her senses dissolved, and that was it.

· · · ·

THIS WAS THE FIFTH time that Deliah had called her mom. She never took this long getting home from the pharmacy, and she had her car with her. Deliah tried to relax, telling herself that her mom had just gone to run a few more errands. She decided to call her dad and let him know what was happening. Maybe he would have better luck.

Deliah's younger siblings, Paxton and Tonia, were zoning out in front of the T.V.

"You guys?" she called, but they ignored her. She rolled her eyes and went into the kitchen. She began pulling out ingredients to make dinner when there was a whooshing sound, followed by Paxton and Tonia's screams.

"What?! What is it?!" Deliah asked as she ran into the living room. A coating of ashes had exploded onto the carpet from the fireplace. "Are you kidding me? What did you do?"

"Nothing," Paxton said. "It just burst out, like - like a Giant blew it out from the flue or something." Tonia nodded her agreement.

Deliah threw her head back in frustration. She walked carefully toward the fireplace to take a look. "Umm . . . It's too dark to see anything." She turned toward her sister and said, "Tonia, go get the flashlight." But Tonia remained where she was.

"D-Deliah . . ." she stammered. She pointed a shaky finger at the fireplace.

Smoke was rising from the unlit hearth; dense and dark like the universe robbed of all light, and life. "Ahh!" Deliah shrieked, swatting it away. As she backed up it seemed to grow thicker, swirling around her like it was trying to trap her.

"Guys, outside now!" she shouted.

She, Paxton, and Tonia ran toward the front door. They tried to open it but the locks were stuck, as if the internal mechanisms had become welded together. When they turned around to go for the back door, their path was blocked; but not by the sinister, revolting fumes. By a girl.

"AHHHH!!!" they screamed.

And in one bizarre moment the situation became even more alarming. The girl started to dance, and as she did Deliah felt a soreness take hold of her insides. There was a pain in her chest, then she abruptly dropped to the floor. Her limbs jerked around like her nerves were being ripped apart, and she felt like her bones were being ground up, like chalk against asphalt. Tonia fell against the door, and Paxton dropped to his knees. Deliah saw that they were experiencing similar symptoms as herself.

Paxton was coughing so heavily that his airway felt like it was full of needles. Blood ran thickly with each heave as he threw up bits of his organs. He fell on his side and grasped at his chest, his body twitching. His throat began to swell and he scratched at his neck. His heart slithered from his mouth, dark and shiny, then he shuddered to a stop.

"Pax . . ." Deliah cried.

Tonia's eyes were shut tightly, and her lungs seemed to shrink, every breath feeling like a barbed wire. She felt like her heart was on fire, and the feeling traveled through to the rest of her body. Her chest became hot, and when she touched it her skin pulled away, sticking to her fingers like melting plastic. Deliah tried to put an arm around her, wanting to protect her from this insane nightmare but woefully unprepared.

After a few more seconds, it didn't matter.

Chapter 9

AFTER SHE PRETENDED to lose consciousness, the little girl was taken to the hospital.

On one level, she could hear the panic-stricken voices of the man and the woman who had helped her. She could feel the hands of the people who had come to transport her. She even remembered the look in Edit's eyes when she had stared directly at him, her purpose almost achieved. What none of them knew is that on another level she was awake.

Deep underground she was sitting on a patch of elevated earth, and everything below her abdominals was consumed by a scarlet fog. Sitting across from her was a woman.

Have you found them?

"I've found one."

That won't be a problem, one will lead you to the other. Where are they taking you?

"To a hospital. They think I'm sick and need help."

Good. They'll take you into their care. They won't suspect anything, but . . . She looked pensively into the little girl's eyes. *What is it?* she asked, betraying a hint of annoyance.

"I think someone does suspect. There's a girl."

On the outside the woman seemed composed, but on the inside she was tense, like a predator about to strike. When she finally spoke, she said with a ruthless certainty, *Be* very *careful. She is the only one who can stop you. And we won't have that.*

• • • •

DURING HER HOSPITAL stay, the girl and the woman conversed. She was told to remain in her comatose state until they could hear what was to happen.

She was lying in a bed, in a little white room. There was a woman hovering over her. Just outside, two people were talking.

"We need to operate on her," Dr. Penn was saying.

"Please, can we just have some time to think about this? We don't even know her name," Athena replied, the concern in her voice prominent.

"She doesn't *have* time," Dr. Penn said forcefully. "Right now you're her only known guardian, and we need your permission to go forward."

Athena looked through the door's window at the sad little girl in her disfigured body. She wanted to help, but there was no guarantee that an operation would even work. And if she didn't act, the girl would be lost anyway. . . .

"This is her best chance, Ms. Harlow."

"I just . . ." Athena turned dejectedly away from the window and said, without much choice, "Okay. . . ."

And that was when the girl received her first instruction: *Don't let them touch you.*

Immediately after the words had been spoken, she opened her eyes.

"Oh, my god," the nurse monitoring her whispered. She opened the door slowly and motioned for Dr. Penn to come inside; Athena followed, pushing her way in. Dr. Penn looked annoyed, but she said nothing. Maybe having Athena in the room would get the girl to share her story. And it did. For two minutes.

She revealed that her name was Abeni, pronounced ah-beh-nee; but when asked about her parents or where she was from, she would only say that her mother was dead.

Dr. Penn was having a difficult time with her new patient. Abeni refused to let her near, even with Athena's help. And when Dr. Penn tried to make it clear that she was in charge, Abeni gave no response; instead, she closed her eyes. She got a look on her face like she was concentrating on something.

You need to get out of here.

. . . .

IT WAS CLOSE TO MIDNIGHT. Athena and Barry had been sent home a few hours before, while Abeni was left overnight in the hospital.

Dr. Penn had stayed with her for almost an hour, trying to gain her trust. She tried to explain what would happen during the procedure, but failed to control her impatience and was met with silence. Finally, she decided that her time would be better spent making sure her surgical team was ready.

Abeni's surgery was scheduled for early in the morning, and while the staff was preparing, she was healing herself.

The swollen areas on her body were reducing. Her cuts were fading into small, white scratches. Her hair was growing back, long and bountiful. Her thin, sickly frame was filling out. Even the hole in her cheek seemed to be knitting itself together.

"You're not in charge, Dr. Penn," she said to herself. "And you don't control me."

. . . .

THE NEXT MORNING, THE surgical team was left baffled and useless; they stared disbelievingly at the newly-healed miracle of a child. Dr. Penn sent one of them away to find out where Abeni had gone and who this new girl was. She didn't appreciate being fooled like this.

"You and your friend are in big trouble," she said as she walked up to the girl; but when she looked into her eyes, she recognized the same steadfast indifference from the night before.

"Oh, my god . . ."

. . . .

ATHENA RUSHED TO THE hospital. She felt guilty about leaving Abeni alone in the care of Dr. Penn, whom she didn't trust.

When she arrived, her feelings of suspicion only increased. For a while, no one seemed to want to tell her anything about Abeni's condition. Finally, Dr. Penn's own assistant was called to escort her to Abeni's room, and when Athena saw her she nearly fell to her knees; Abeni was looking much better, like she had never been hurt in the first place.

As usual she was fighting Dr. Penn, who now wanted her to stay so that her immune system could be studied to benefit others. And although she did not want to admit it, Dr. Penn was frustrated at not being able to discover the cause of Abeni's uncommon healing process.

Athena hated the idea of Abeni being dissected to please Dr. Penn's ego; she fought back, making it clear that she would just take Abeni if she had to.

While she and Dr. Penn argued, Abeni received a new instruction: *Give me control!*

In the middle of her sentence, Dr. Penn's demeanor changed. Her eyes became unfocused, and when her assistant spoke to her she had difficulty responding. She was able, suddenly, to decide that Abeni needed only a few cautionary checks.

And half an hour later she was signed out of the hospital, officially discharged and on her way back to Harlow's.

Chapter 10

EDIT FINISHED WASHING the dishes. He wiped the sink, then went to help with whatever he could in the living room. He had been operating like a robot, lifeless and automatic, ever since he had heard the news: Abeni was coming home.

Artemis had helped the kids to put on their best clothes, and now they were waiting quietly in the living room. Ellis and Aphrodite were prepping a special lunch. Dina was organizing books and toys. Ambrose spoke to the kids, reassuring them that Abeni was fine and it would be nice to have her at Harlow's. Everyone was trying to handle their jitters, but Edit felt dreadful, like his judgement day was approaching with an unfavorable verdict. And poor little Mira hadn't spoken to anyone all morning. Not even him.

Artemis walked into the living room, excited but as nervous as everyone else. "They're almost here. Is everyone ready?"

No one answered, but the kids tried to sit up a little straighter. Five minutes later they heard the jingle of keys, then Athena walked in with Abeni holding her hand.

"Hi, Abeni," Artemis said. "Welcome home." She motioned for the kids to come greet their new family member - Mira stayed as far back as possible - then Abeni was introduced to the caregivers. When she got to Edit he could feel his eyes wanting to look away, and when he tried to speak his mouth had gone dry.

"Um . . . Hi, Abeni. W-Welcome to Harlow's."

"Thanks."

After introductions an intensely awkward quietness took over, so Athena said, a little louder than she meant to, "Okay, how about we all take a few minutes? Abeni, we'll make you some breakfast. After that, Artemis will take you to meet your theater group. Sound good?"

"Okay," Abeni said, her face emotionless. Athena smiled a bit sadly, then went into the kitchen; Artemis and Aphrodite close behind her.

Some of the kids began getting over their nervousness, but they were far from comfortable with this newcomer. She made no attempt to speak to them, and no one was quite sure what to do. Dina tried to help by sitting the kids in a circle and having them talk a bit about themselves. Mira stayed with Edit.

They pulled out some pencils and paper and began sketching random thoughts. Mira whispered so quietly that Edit almost thought he'd imagined her words, "She's dangerous. We can't trust her."

Edit glanced at the kids seated in their uneven circle, talking and laughing quietly. "What is it?" he whispered back.

Mira looked like she was concentrating deeply on something. "She's lying about some things, or there are things she isn't saying. I heard Athena tell Artemis and Aphrodite that her mother died, but . . . I don't know. It's . . . There's something in her eyes." Edit shivered. Again with those eyes. "But there is one thing. . . ." Mira said hesitantly.

"What?" Edit asked, though he was sure he didn't want to know.

"She . . . she wants something from you, but I don't know what, and I don't know why at all."

"*Wants* something?" Edit asked, nearly forgetting to whisper. He felt his heartbeat speed up slightly. "Mira . . . this makes *no* sense-"

"I know," she said sadly. "There's something around her, like a dark cloud. Look, Edit, just stay away from her, okay? Don't go near her at all."

Edit nodded. "Okay."

He had already decided that he would do whatever he could to avoid Abeni. Although . . . part of him felt like she couldn't be avoided, no matter how much he wished it.

After things had settled a bit, Artemis gathered the kids together. As they were lining up she said, "Okay, let's see . . . Dina? Edit? Why don't you two come with us today."

Chapter 11

MIRA USUALLY STAYED home during theater trips. She didn't like the idea of being compared to other kids to see what she could do; she knew what she was capable of, and that was good enough for her. But after Edit's name had been called she jumped up, the action occurring as a reflex, and insisted on coming too. Now she was at the back of the group, holding tightly to his hand and keeping a close watch on Abeni.

When they entered the lobby, they were directed by the front desk manager into the auditorium, where Kent Verne was waiting for them. Kent was a local actor, Artemis's best friend since elementary school, and the owner of The Juvenescence Theater.

"Hey, guys," he said as they walked into the auditorium.

Dina and Edit seated themselves in the first row with the kids, while Artemis took Abeni onstage and introduced her to Kent. He asked her many questions, and Mira wished she could hear what they were saying, but the other kids had decided to become loud and rowdy.

"Ughh. Couldn't they choose another time to do this?" Mira groaned.

"Relax, doesn't look like there's anything wrong. Besides, what can she possibly do here? An auditorium? - that's thinking small for a conquest of world domination," Edit whispered. Mira gave a small smile, but Edit could see that she just wasn't in a joking mood. And the truth was, her earlier words had scared him. He was trying to lighten things up for himself as much as for her.

They sat quietly for a few minutes, then Edit got up to settle a minor squabble. A classic: Reyna and Julian were fighting over the joint armrest. Edit exchanged some words with Dina, then jogged out of the auditorium.

Kent made a call to someone. "She'll be down in a little bit," he said to Artemis and Abeni. A few minutes later, Ms. Alanna, one of the dance teachers walked in.

"Hello, everyone," she said cheerfully, waving both hands.

"Oh, Anna, there you are," Kent greeted her. He introduced her to Abeni. She seemed to get along well with Ms. Alanna, better than she had with anyone else.

While the two got to work, Mira shuddered suddenly. She looked around, her eyebrows furrowed, like she was trying to find something important. Were those . . . *voices*? But besides the group in the seats, and the four onstage, there were no others in the auditorium. Mira's roaming eyes stopped on Abeni. One of the voices was coming from her.

Square your hips . . . Drop your shoulders . . . Wing your foot . . .

"What? What is that?" Mira whispered. The voice was unfamiliar to her, but the ones which followed she felt like she knew somehow.

ENTER THE MIND WITH CAUTION, MIRA. FOR NOW SHE IS DISTRACTED, BUT IF SHE GETS THE CHANCE, SHE MAY TRY TO COME AFTER YOU.

"Who?" Mira asked, but the voices were gone. She was back in the auditorium with her noisy family.

When Edit returned, his pouch-converted shirt was carrying snacks from the lobby vending machines. He handed Mira a bottle of strawberry-flavored milk and a pack of peanut butter sandwich crackers. She didn't take them right away. It was occurring to her that she had just entered Abeni's mind, but it wasn't her voice that had spoken. And those other voices . . . where had they come from?

"Mira? What's up?" Edit asked, sounding concerned.

Mira stayed silent for a minute longer, then: "Edit . . . there's something different here. It's coming from her."

Edit looked at Abeni, who was practicing dance steps with Ms. Alanna. They looked like they were working out a routine. "What do you mean different?"

"I think it's the auditorium – no, wait. It's more like . . . it's more like the stage. It's like she's . . . happier? At least, comfortable or something. . . ." She sounded lost, like her mind journey had weakened her focus.

Edit found it difficult to look away from the bits of footwork that Abeni was practicing. Today the fire in her was one of artistic passion, and he began to wonder if she was so dangerous after all.

"You can't fall for her tricks, Edit!" Mira whispered sharply, reading his expression. "There's something wrong with her, I know it!"

Edit was surprised by her intensity. "Sorry. You're right, it's just . . ." he wasn't sure what it was that he even meant to say, but it didn't matter. Ms. Alanna was calling for everyone's attention.

"Ladies and gentlemen, I introduce your newest rising star in the world of dance: Abeni."

For the next two minutes, everyone was entranced. Abeni kept her audience in such wondrous rapture that for a moment even Mira almost debated her threat potential. At the end of her performance there was a silence which lasted for two eight counts. Ms. Alanna had tears in her eyes. Then all at once, the congratulatory sound of applause broke out, the support from the small group magnified by their enthusiasm.

After the applause died down, Ms. Alanna asked breathlessly, "Abeni . . . where did you learn to dance?"

Abeni's face was neutral, but Mira could sense a shift under the surface. Abeni shrugged and said, "I was taught by the greatest."

Chapter 12

IDA LOOKED UP FROM her book as her aunt pulled into the driveway. She jumped up to meet her, but stopped when she noticed the odd look on her aunt's face. "Aunty Kae? What happened? Are you all right?" she asked. She put down her book and waited for her aunt to speak.

"I don't know, I think . . . On my way here I think I almost ran over someone." She sounded unsure, like she was struggling to remember if the event had even occurred.

"Oh, my god! Well, what happened?! Are you okay?! What happened to the other person?"

Kae shook her head slowly. "I . . . I think I might have imagined the whole thing. I just . . . can't seem to remember."

Ida's concern shifted to suspicion. "Aunty Kae . . . you haven't been drinking again, have you?"

"What? No, no, no!"

Just to be sure, Ida inspected her aunt's car. She found no alcohol, but she did find souvenirs from her aunt's hiking trip. Relieved, she asked, "So how was your trip?"

Kae smiled as she recalled the scene. "It was . . . incredible. I think you would have liked it, Ida. At sunset the mountains lit up, like a rainbow-colored fire. The air was like, crisp and wild and kind of smoky, but not like your dad's nasty cigarettes. I felt like a character in one of your books."

"Hmm. Sounds cool, but I think I'll stick to reading about adventures."

They laughed and went into the house.

• • • •

"AUNTY KAE!" NASH SAID excitedly as she walked into the kitchen. He was perhaps the most thrilled to see her, as they were both adopted. He put down a stack of plates and hugged her.

The back door swung open and Kae's little brother Kian walked in. "Ah, I thought I heard your car," he said. His hands, face, and clothes were dusted in ashes from the firepit.

"Um, I think you missed a spot," Kae joked.

"Typical," Kian said as he rolled his eyes. "Hey, you guys almost done with dinner?"

"Yeah, just about," Nash replied. "We just need to set the table." He started handing plates and utensils to his sister.

"And while we're doing this," Kae said as she washed her hands to help, "you can go and hose yourself off." Everyone chuckled at her lame joke.

"Typical," Kian said again as he went upstairs to clean up.

• • • •

AFTER DINNER, THEY sat around the firepit and relaxed with some roasted marshmallows.

The night was warm and peaceful. Kae was telling everyone about her trip. Ida was only half-listening. She was eager to get back to her book, wondering about how it might end, when she thought she noticed movement outside the light of the fire.

Spots popped in her eyes as she blinked and tried to focus on some shadows in the trees. Yes, there it was, something moving in the darkness. Ida kept watching, and in another minute the figure stepped out from the shadows. It was a girl.

Huh? Ida thought.

"What is it, Ida?" Nash asked, noticing the strange look on his sister's face. She pointed to the girl, who had now walked into the middle of the street.

Kian stood up and called, "Hey, what are you doing, kid?" She didn't respond. "Little girl? Can you hear me?" If she could, she was choosing to ignore him.

"Un-freaking-believable," Kian muttered.

"Well, if she won't listen to us, we have to go get her," Kae said, her protective nature surfacing. "What if a car . . . ?" she trailed off. "Wait . . . I think I've seen her before." As Kae tried to remember, the girl started to dance; right there in the street.

The fire began to change. The flames rose a bit higher, yet they gave no warmth. And instead of its bright orange color, the fire darkened, taking on a deep red hue.

"What is going on?" Nash whispered, rubbing his arms.

"Dad, maybe we should call the police," Ida suggested, but her father didn't respond. Instead, he had started coughing, making sounds like he was trying to expel his throat.

"Kian Cornell," Kae said, half-angry, half-worried, "how many *freaking* times have I told you to drop the cigarettes?"

"Dad?" Nash patted his father's back a few times, then walked to the drink cooler to get him some water.

There was a loud gasping sound. Kae and Nash looked at Ida. She was exhaling short, choppy breaths, and patting her chest like something had become lodged inside it.

Nash ran to his sister's side. Kae took out her cellphone to call the police, but even as she dialed the number, Kian gasped like he had just broken the surface of deep water. His heart felt swollen, his body sagging with the weight. He crumpled to the ground, then went still. Ida was shuddering like she was experiencing shocks throughout her body. Her chest caved as if a bowling ball had been dropped on it, then . . . nothing.

· · · ·

SHE CREPT AWAY AS EASILY as she had come. But it wasn't over yet.

Just two remain.

Chapter 13

"GOOD NIGHT," EDIT SAID, and ended the call.

'Investigators are still exploring the mysterious deaths of Harley Brysen and her three children Deliah, Paxton, and Tonia, and Kian Cornell and his daughter Ida Cornell. Due to similarities in both cases, there is some suspicion that these events may be the work of a serial killer-'

Edit shut off the T.V. He had been on edge for the past few days, ever since Abeni had shown up; and learning about the unfortunate fate of those families wasn't helping. He felt like his insides were deteriorating, and if he didn't talk to someone soon he would become physically sick. He called his mom, who answered on the second ring.

"Edit, how are you? How's work? How's Mira doing?"

"Hey, Mom," Edit said, already feeling happier. "I'll be okay. Work is good . . . ish. Mira's been feeling a little tense."

"Edit, you don't sound okay. What do you mean good-ish? And what's happened to Mira? Is this about Abeni?"

Edit had told his parents about the new arrival. He couldn't explain everything, but he did mention that the new girl made Mira uncomfortable, and by extension himself.

"Edit, do you think that maybe you're overreacting a bit? Maybe you're still trying to cope with what you saw. I mean, you've *never* reacted this way to a new child at Harlow's."

But she's not just a child, Edit thought miserably. "Well, sure . . . But don't you think it's weird how quickly she recovered? It took her barely a day. And then we find out that she's some dance star prodigy? Mira said – I mean-"

"Edit, I think you're being a little paranoid here. And I don't think it's fair that you're judging her situation without knowing all the facts. I can't explain why she recovered so quickly, and maybe she had friends or a teacher who taught her how to dance. What I'm trying to say is, there are things in her life which only she understands, and if she doesn't want to explain then we can't force her. All we can do is be there for her when she needs us."

"Well . . . yeah, I guess. . . ."

When Edit's mom spoke again he could hear the smile in her voice. "Anyway, have you spoken to Athena yet?"

Edit couldn't help but smile himself. "Yeah, just got off the phone with her, actually. Everything's okay."

"Oh, that's great. I'm so excited, I-"

"Mom?"

Edit's mom remained silent on her end.

"Mom, what's going on?"

"I'm not-" She gasped. She was so surprised that she dropped her phone, but Edit could hear her screaming at something.

"Mom?! What is it?! MOM!!" For about twenty seconds, there was silence. Then a voice came on the line.

"Hi, Edit."

Edit froze. A feeling of dread quivered through his body. He knew that voice, and it should not have been there. "You evil little psycho! What have you done to my mom?! Where is she?!"

"She's fine, but I need you to meet me, or she won't be. Don't waste her time calling for help. At the theater. See you soon."

• • • •

MIRA COULDN'T SLEEP. Something was happening, she could feel it. She got out of bed and crept to Abeni's room. She didn't even knock, but turned the doorknob and peeked inside.

Empty.

Mira's nightmares were suddenly alive; she felt cornered by all the demons that chased her in her sleep. As quietly as she could, she snuck into the kitchen and found the biggest knife there was. She didn't try to push away her fear, but used it as a driving force.

She had to be brave. Edit needed her.

Chapter 14

EDIT RAN WITHOUT STOPPING until he got to the theater. The main doors were open, welcoming him inside like they had been waiting for him. This didn't make him feel any better, but he ran in. He had to.

The theater seemed eerily empty. It was dark and although Edit knew the layout, he had to hold out his arms to guide himself. He stumbled through the lobby, past some of the studios. There was a dim light ahead which helped him find his way. He stepped out of the darkness and through the open doors of the auditorium. There was his mom lying on the stage, still alive but unconscious. She was close to the edge, like she had been purposely placed there.

He was Tantalus and she was the fruit.

"Mom!" Edit started to run to her, but stopped when he saw someone walk out from stage right. He looked around automatically, searching for a weapon. *Damn!* he thought. At least this time he didn't back down, but stared unflinchingly into those poisonous blue eyes.

"Let. Her. Go."

Abeni stared steadily back. "No."

Edit ran forward, charged with a furious adrenaline, ready to jump onto the stage and squeeze his hands around Abeni's neck. When he was just a few feet away something slammed into him, throwing him back halfway to the doors. His head smacked against the floor and his mind turned hazy, as if a thousand simultaneous ripples were vibrating against each other.

"I don't think you should try that again. She's already angry at you and you'll only make it worse," Abeni said indifferently.

Edit leaned on the closest chair and used it to prop himself up. His limbs were shaky, and his mouth felt thick and useless. "What do you mean? . . . And what do you want with my mom? I thought it was me you were after."

"It is. Both of you. And it's not me who's after you."

"Then who?"

"My mother."

Silence pressed against Edit's ears and seemed to expand. It was like a church bell had been rung but no sound was coming out. "Liar . . . Your mom is dead."

"That's right."

"What? . . . Abeni, look, what do you want? Just let my mom go and I'll help you. Please . . . just tell me what you want."

"It's not about what I want, it's about what she wants. And she wants you to die."

Chapter 15

IT WAS NOW ELEVEN YEARS since Celise began her training at Sícone's Dual-Spirit Dance Academy.

However strange people found her, she had grown into a remarkable woman and magnificent dancer, constantly earning recognition from the many prominent roles in her career. But it seemed that her previous triumphs were just the training for the challenge she would soon face; one which, if she succeeded, would begin a new series of greatness in her life.

One woman would be chosen for the principal role in an upcoming original ballet, created by a rising and innovative presence in the industry of the Performing Arts: Director, Ira Auberon. The chosen dancer would also get the chance to train and perform in one of the most renowned birth places of dance: Paris.

Overseeing the audition were Signeus Lamont, head of the Parisian dance academy to be featured; Deon Cornell, producer of the ballet; and Ira Auberon himself.

"Ladies, good morning and welcome," he began. He went on to explain his vision, and talked about the rigorous tests which those who advanced would face.

"Be prepared," he said seriously. "This will not be like any audition you have ever attended."

· · · ·

BY THE END OF THE FIRST day, three dancers had been cut. By the second day, four more had been let go; and by the next, another two resigned. On the final day only two dancers remained: Celise Bromwell, and Mavis Hamilton.

The judges were aware of Celise's reputation and excited to have her as a finalist. Mavis, although not as well-known, commanded her own kind of excellence.

She was noticeably nervous while waiting for the judges to deliberate; and truthfully, she was a little afraid of Celise. She had heard about the incident from eleven years ago with Sobrina, and about a few other things which made her wary of her competitor.

Celise composed herself calmly and professionally. She kept her hands laced behind her, back straight, and chin up. Her eyes did not stray from the judges. They exchanged some last words; finally, Mr. Auberon stood.

"Ladies, I want to commend you on your completion of this audition, and I want to personally thank you for your work, talent, and passion for this inspirational art. It is unfortunate that we may only select one of you, but we have decided that the lead will be played by . . . Miss Hamilton."

There was a hesitant silence. Mavis was sure that she had heard incorrectly, but the words resounded long and loudly in Celise's ears.

In a moment, a flood of relief rushed from Mavis's eyes. Mr. Auberon couldn't stop the warm smile that softened his face; it was truly heartwarming to see her so tenderly happy. When she calmed down, he addressed her.

"Congratulations, Miss Hamilton," he said. Mavis thanked him, still shocked but elated.

Mr. Auberon then addressed Celise. "Miss Bromwell . . . you are undoubtedly a woman of notability in your craft. I know that my words must seem hollow in a moment such as this, but I must say how sincerely sorry I – that *we* are, that we could not choose you today."

No.

But they would be.

Chapter 16

AFTER DISCUSSING PREPARATIONS with Mr. Auberon, Mr. Lamont, and Mr. Cornell, Mavis went to the changing room. She was packing up her belongings and thinking about her upcoming trip. She had not stopped smiling since her name had been called, and couldn't wait to get home to share the news with her parents.

"Congratulations."

"Ah!" Mavis spun around, surprised by who had spoken. "Oh . . . Oh, Celise. Thank you. I'm sorry I yelled, I . . ." She took a tentative step forward. "You were so quiet, I didn't hear you come in."

"I know."

Celise approached Mavis with a menacing gait.

"What . . . What are you doing?" she asked, her voice trembling.

Instead of responding Celise pulled back her arm, and before Mavis could scream she swung it down with the force of a catapult. Mavis's body slumped to the floor, strips of her eliminated face hanging from Celise's nails.

She examined the body, trying to decide where to begin. She knelt down by Mavis's ankles and yanked them from her legs, then broke the feet in half. Splinters of bone and pieces of muscle erupted like lava from a volcano.

She stepped on Mavis's knees one at a time, then wrenched the legs upward. The resulting snap gave her a feeling of perverse ecstasy. She finished by ripping Mavis's thighs from their sockets, tugging at them like they were a stubborn, fibrous grouping of weeds.

Her hands and arms were covered in crimson, her face and clothes spotted with shiny splotches of red. She looked at Mavis's body, strewn across the floor like butchered samples of beef.

No one would ever again recognize her.

Celise placed a hand on her own chest and felt her heart bubbling underneath, like boiling water. She wasn't finished, and she was running out of time. She walked out of the changing room, broke through a window, and went home.

Chapter 17

MRS. BROMWELL WAS FRANTIC when she arrived at the Audition Hall. Her head felt like it was on fire, and when people spoke to her their voices echoed and sounded far away. She heard a commotion in the direction of the changing room and followed it. She found Mr. Auberon, Mr. Lamont, and Mr. Cornell distraught over a woman's mutilated body. When they finally noticed her, they tried to shield her from the sadistic scene, but she pushed them away. She had just one thought in her mind.

"Where is my daughter?" She walked right up to Mr. Auberon. *"Where is Celise?"*

"Mrs. Bromwell . . . we don't know where your daughter is. We never saw her again after the audition."

"What do you mean?" Mrs. Bromwell demanded.

"At the conclusion of the audition we chose . . . Your daughter was not chosen for our part. She seemed a bit . . . frozen. I spoke to her, but she never responded, just curtsied and walked away. I-"

Mrs. Bromwell held up her hand, cutting him off. And in a tone that scorched the air she said, "What have you done!"

. . . .

CELISE FELT LIKE SHE had been walking for days; really, she was a gust of wind bolting past the people on the sidewalks. Their eyes just hinted at a streak of red and white before it left them far behind.

When Celise got home she threw open the doors. No one came out to challenge her. To her room she walked, as if in a trance, and picked up her jewelry box. She carried it upstairs to the private room on the fifth floor. Mrs. Bromwell had given her the only key, and, following tradition, Scarlett's diary.

Celise unlocked the door and stepped inside. She set her jewelry box on the floor, then took the diary from its shelf, stumbling as she did. Again she touched her chest, and this time she could feel her heart chipping away, like an old porcelain vase.

She opened the diary to the last empty page and began to write.

Mother,

I have only a few minutes to speak to you, and you won't see me again for a while. Find me in Ginen, I will be waiting for you there. I have a plan and I will need yours and everyone else's help to complete it. They took something from me – now I will take EVERYTHING from them.

Celise Adair.

Celise closed the diary and opened the jewelry box. She removed the padding to uncover a secret compartment, and inside was a dagger which had belonged to her grandmother. She removed her bodice, exposing the skin above her heart, and positioned the dagger.

"Great-grandmother Scarlett, I shall soon be with you."

· · · ·

MRS. BROMWELL HEARD the torturous screams of her daughter from a block away. She had taken control of the carriage reins, but she could not urge those horses to move fast enough.

· · · ·

USING THE STRENGTH of her ancestors, Celise made a deep cut into her chest, hacking away the flesh until she uncovered her heart. She reaped it out with the dagger and just had time to place it inside the jewelry box. The fire in her eyes was lessening, the color now a dim blue, but it had not been extinguished; that fire would burn again.

She fell over just as her mother made it upstairs, wailing for her daughter's life.

Chapter 18

CELISE'S FAMILY HELD a private funeral for her at their home. She was laid in a coffin built to resemble her music box, and a few days later was joined by her mother.

During the short time in which Mrs. Bromwell outlived her daughter, she carried the box containing her heart, and Scarlett's diary. Both had been buried with her.

· · · ·

WHEN MRS. BROMWELL opened her eyes, she saw only darkness. She was falling down a hole – no, more like a canyon. After what seemed like a hundred years, she thought she could make out some color. It started out as a dark gray, slightly lighter than the walls which surrounded her, then it shifted into a deep red.

When Mrs. Bromwell finally reached the bottom, she was standing in a layer of fog that engulfed every direction. Thick curls of smothering softness fell from a visible height of three stories, coating the walls in red, wispy waterfalls. Mrs. Bromwell could see nothing below her knees, and when she looked up there was only the everlasting darkness of the canyon. She knew where she was, Celise's heart had guided her.

And as if the heart had called to its Master, Celise came forward; and Mrs. Bromwell heard the voice she had been aching to hear since it had been taken from her.

"Hello, Mother," Celise said. Her hair had been released from its usual neat bun, and now it rippled down her back. She wore a white dress that disappeared into the foggy ground. Mrs. Bromwell was dressed similarly, her hair in a likewise fashion.

"Celise," she said, the name barely a whisper from her lips. "What is your plan?"

Celise raised a hand and more figures began to appear from the smoky walls, outfitted as she and her mother were. Mrs. Bromwell recognized her own mother, her grandmother, and her great-grandmother. She knew that the others were the previous women in the Adair line.

One was taller than the rest, like a delicate little Giantess. She was clearly the eldest, and her face was tricky and mischievous.

"Scarlett," Mrs. Bromwell said.

The woman smiled a big but uninviting smile. "Hello, Devona. Thank you for keeping my diary." She addressed the other women assembled. "And thank all of you for passing on my gift." They bowed; Celise and Mrs. Bromwell did the same.

"Now, Celise, what is it you need from us?" Scarlett asked.

Celise stared at her, for once a bit overwhelmed. This was the woman who had made her what she was. "Great-grandmother Scarlett, I need a way to reach the visible world and collect what is owed to me."

Scarlett smiled again in that alluring, lethal way. "Then you will have it."

The women arranged themselves in a circle with Celise in the center. Scarlett began to pray to her spirits. The abyss shook and the smoky waterfalls became distorted, breaking their downward path.

In front of Celise the fog began to churn, weaving together to create a vessel, like a mannequin of a young girl. Each of the women stepped forward, placed a hand above the vessel, and spoke a prayer.

Scarlett looked pleased with the work. She looked at Mrs. Bromwell and said, "The only thing which remains is a life force."

Mrs. Bromwell looked at Celise as if asking for permission; when Celise nodded, she removed the heart from its case and placed it into the chest of the vessel. It began to grow features; Celise's hair, nose, eyes, and lips. It acquired Celise's abilities, her strength. The fog clung to it, becoming a black skirted leotard. The vessel opened its eyes and stood, and the first woman it looked at was Celise.

"Your name is Abeni," she said. "You are now my weapon. You will return to the visible world and end the blood of those who wronged me. Do exactly as you are told until you find and eliminate your targets: Harley, Deliah, Paxton, and Tonia Lamont; Kian and Ida Cornell; and Wynn and Edit Auberon."

Chapter 19

"WHY? . . . WHY ARE you doing this?" Edit asked.

"You and your mother are descendants of Ira Auberon. You took away my mother's life. Now she's going to take yours."

"Took your mother's . . . ?" Edit said in disbelief. The more he tried to understand, the more disconnected he felt.

"Ahhh . . ." he groaned, placing a trembling hand on his forehead. He felt like his head was being split open, and something was tunneling through the crack into his brain.

You don't have to fight anymore, he thought, but he hadn't done so on his own. *It's okay. You can be free.* It was like his thoughts were being prompted by someone else.

You've felt like giving up before. Why not just let go?

"Yeah . . . yeah, maybe . . . " Edit said, the words stumbling from his mouth. He heard his mom moan. She was starting to move, trying to wake up. Even after being knocked out and kidnapped, she still had power in her to fight. She was much stronger than Edit had realized in all the time he had known her. And it wasn't just her.

Edit's parents had done everything for him, always trying to make sure that he became the very best of himself. And the Harlow sisters, taking it upon themselves to care for people who needed help the most. And the caregivers; they were true friends, a reliable team whom many people depended on.

"No . . . You're wrong," Edit said. "I do have to fight. And I will."

Then you will suffer!

The auditorium seemed to sway. The walls were undulating almost imperceptibly. The lights flickered in slow motion and became irritatingly bright.

Abeni took up a position. There was no music, no audience, but that didn't matter. Tonight, she was dancing for her mother's life, dancing to take another's.

Wynn felt it first. She creaked her eyes open and they were hit by bright lights from far above. A feeling of thickness crushed her head, and her body throbbed like the resounding tones of a gong. Her eyes adjusted to the glare and she recognized the auditorium of The Juvenescence Theater. And there in the aisle, leaning on one of the rows. Was that . . . ?

"Edit . . ."

As Wynn tried to crawl to him, her breath was snatched from her lungs. She stopped, and her body crumpled from the sudden change. She heard her son scream.

· · · ·

"AHHHHH!!!" EDIT'S ANKLES shattered, as if tiny bombs had been detonated inside them. He fell, landing on his wrists, and his veins popped like firecrackers.

Abeni performed a series of turns, and Wynn screamed as invisible knives zig-zagged across her torso.

"Mom . . ." Edit tried to crawl to her, using his elbows to pull himself forward. His legs dragged uselessly behind and the movement only amplified the agony. His limbs began to curl and twist up, like stiff, worn-out pieces of elastic.

Wynn was blacking out in a span of seconds. She knew she was dying, and all she could do was watch as her son shared in her fate. A girl leaped over her and onto the floor. It was the same girl who had appeared in her apartment.

Skin as white as marble, and probably just as cold. Black hair, so shiny it was almost iridescent, fashioned in an elaborate bun at the nape of her neck. Clothes that flowed and swirled like smoke when she moved. And eyes as sharp as the fear shooting through Wynn's body.

Finally, her heart burst. Her surroundings blurred into randomness, then it was over.

Abeni finished dancing. She walked around Edit's broken body, examining him as if making sure that she had done her job correctly.

Edit saw his mom stop moving. In his brain he couldn't believe that it had happened, but from his eyes the tears streamed out, some falling into his open mouth. He was able to turn his head enough to look up at Abeni's blank face, and he became as angry as he did when he first ran into the theater. As a last act of defiance he glared at her, his eyes spitting out their own fiery wrath. They moved to a spot behind her, then she gasped.

A large knife had been plunged through Abeni's back and out her chest, and skewered on the end of it was her heart.

The force of the impact pushed her forward. As she fell, her body broke apart, trailing behind her in long, stringy wisps, until it disappeared into the height of the ceiling. The knife now without a target clattered to the floor, already disintegrating from the unknown caustic substance.

Mira dropped beside Edit, the strength drained from her body. Through her tears, she could see her misery reflected on his face. She knelt by his head and rested it on her lap, and when she did, his pain lessened and he was able to think.

He thought about the moment that he had found her; the birthday celebrations on her assumed birth date; the snowball fight they had had; the wonderful pictures he had taught her how to create; the feeling that they were father and daughter. He thought about the years that he had raised her until this moment. He would not leave this world in pain.

"I'm sorry, Edit," Mira cried. "I'm sorry I couldn't save you."

Edit couldn't speak; he shook his head very gently, as if saying to her: *I know you tried.*

Mira understood. Her tears fell more freely, catching up with each other before they rolled off her face, and obscuring the moment when Edit left her.

Chapter 20

"WE'VE GOT TWO BODIES and a little girl," Mira heard the Police Officer saying into his radio. She was sitting in the back of his patrol car, like a ghost without a purpose, staring at nothing.

There was so much commotion outside; people shouting, police sirens, and now Athena running up to join the disarray, her face twisted with grief and worry. But Mira didn't notice any of it, or didn't have the strength to care. She had failed, and now her family was dead.

The police believed that this was a third attack from their suspected serial killer. Like in the other killings, a family member had been left alive. Bennett Samuel, husband to Wynn and father to Edit, seemed to have no knowledge of what had happened.

All he remembered is that he had been tired last night, more so than usual. His wife had received a call from their son, and a few moments later he went to bed. He woke up the next morning in time to answer the knocking of police officers at his door. It took him a long time to get there; he felt groggy, and with every wobble had to steady himself against a wall or a piece of furniture. When he heard the news, he was further convinced that he was having a nightmare.

Athena believed that Mira had suffered some sort of mental shock. The only thing she would say is that Abeni had killed Edit and Wynn, and if she had stopped her in time Edit and Wynn would still be alive.

The biggest problem with Mira's explanation is that there was no Abeni.

There never had been.

• • • •

THE HARLOW SISTERS hosted a funeral service for Edit and Wynn; just Bennett, the caregivers, and the kids.

It was a surreal affair, especially for Bennett. In one night he had lost his wife and his son in a suspected string of homicides, and more than once he found himself wondering if any of it was even real.

He spoke about how his son struggled to feel fulfilled in his life; how his place at Harlow's gave him a purpose. He spoke about Wynn's inspirational tendency to try to see others as they were. His words began to deteriorate as his feelings took over, so he ended by donating the finished charcoal piece that he had found in Edit's apartment.

After everyone said their pieces, no one felt much like doing anything. For the kids, seeing all these distraught adults, the people who had rescued them from their calamity and heartache, was too much. Mostly, everyone came together and just hugged.

Athena took Mira aside and they sat down together in a corner of the room. Mira didn't try to resist; she didn't want to. After her interview she had said almost nothing for days. Athena decided it would be best to just get to the point.

"He, um . . . he was going to adopt you."

For the first time in days, Mira responded to something, snapping her head up to look Athena in the eyes.

"I was talking to him that night, before . . . We were going to surprise you with it. He . . . He was so nervous when he came to me about it." She chuckled sadly. "I've known Edit for a long time. He found it hard to worry much about himself. It's like Bennett said, I think it helped him to do things for others . . . for you kids. . . . I absolutely trust that he . . . he would have been the *perfect* dad for you."

And the only one I wanted, Mira thought. She hugged Athena for a long time. "Thanks, Athena. Thanks for telling me."

Athena nodded. She could tell that Mira wanted to be alone.

Mira sat at the table that she and Edit had shared over a week ago. "If only I could have saved you, things would be different. If only I could have saved you. . . ."

But . . . maybe she could.

Mira knew that she wasn't like the other kids, and neither was Abeni - but they were like each other. Mira sensed things that others couldn't. She was the only one who could remember that Abeni had existed. And those voices in her head, they were the same kind that had been in Abeni's.

Something had happened to Abeni that had made her what she was. Maybe the same thing had happened to Mira.

What if she could figure it out? Maybe there was a way.

Don't miss out!

Visit the website below and you can sign up to receive emails whenever T. B. Vera publishes a new book. There's no charge and no obligation.

https://books2read.com/r/B-A-UIKG-CCDW

BOOKS 2 READ

Connecting independent readers to independent writers.